Alexander, Who's Not
(*Do you hear me? I mean it!*)
Going to Move

JUDITH VIORST

illustrated by
Robin Preiss Glasser
in the style of Ray Cruz

ALADDIN PAPERBACKS

*The author and publisher gratefully acknowledge Ray Cruz,
not only as the talented artist who first brought Alexander
to life visually, but also for his contributions to the
initial development of art for this book, which, for
personal reasons, he could not complete. His spirit of
cooperation and his generous concern for the enjoyment of
young readers deserve the highest praise.*

First Aladdin Paperback edition August 1998

Text copyright © 1995 by Judith Viorst
Illustrations copyright ©1995 by Robin Preiss Glasser

Aladdin Paperbacks
An imprint of Simon & Schuster Children's Publishing Division
1230 Avenue of the Americas
New York, New York 10020

The text of this book is set in Plantin Light
Manufactured in China

16 18 20 19 17

Library of Congress has catalogued the hardcover edition as follows:
Viorst, Judith
Alexander, who's not (do you hear me? I mean it!) going to move / Judith Viorst; illustrated by Robin Preiss Glasser.—1st ed.
p. cm.
Summary: Angry Alexander refuses to move away if it means having to leave his favorite friends and special places.
ISBN-13: 978-0-689-31958-7 (hc.)
ISBN-10: 0-689-31958-4 (hc.)
[1. Moving, Household—Fiction.] I. Preiss Glasser, Robin, ill. II. Title.
PZ7.V816A11 1995
[E]—dc20
95-5277
CIP AC
ISBN-13: 978-0-689-82089-2 (Aladdin pbk.)
ISBN-10: 0-689-82089-5 (Aladdin pbk.)

For Miranda Rachel Viorst

—J.V.

For my sister Erica, who has always been there for me

—R.P.G.

They can't make me pack my baseball mitt or my I LOVE DINOSAURS
sweatshirt or my cowboy boots. They can't make me pack my ice skates,
my jeans with eight zippers, my compass, my radio or my stuffed pig.
My dad is packing. My mom is packing.
My brothers Nick and Anthony are packing.

I'm not packing. I'm not going to move.

My dad says we have to move to where his new job is. That job is a thousand miles away. My mom says we have to move to where our new house is. That house is a thousand miles away. Right next door to the new house there's a boy who is Anthony's age. Down the street there's a boy the same age as Nick.

There's no one next door or down the street or maybe for a thousand miles who is my age.

I'm not—DO YOU HEAR ME? I MEAN IT!—going to move.

I'll never have a best friend like Paul again. I'll never have a great sitter like Rachel again. I'll never have my soccer team or my car pool again. I'll never have kids who know me, except my brothers, and sometimes *they* don't want to know me.

I'm not packing. I'm not going to move.

Nick says I'm a fool and should get a brain transplant. Anthony says I'm being immature. My mom and my dad say that after a while I'll get used to living a thousand miles from everything.

Never. Not ever. No way. Uh uh. N. O.

I maybe could stay here
and live with the Baldwins.
They've got a dog.

I always wanted a dog.

I maybe could stay here and live with the Rooneys. They've got six girls. They always wanted one boy.

I maybe could stay here and live with Mr. and Mrs. Oberdorfer.
They always give great treats on Halloween.

I maybe could stay here
and live by myself in maybe
a tree house or maybe a
tent or maybe a cave.

Nick says I could live in the zoo with all the other animals.
Anthony says I'm being immature. My dad says I should take a last
look at all my special places.

I'm taking a look—but it won't be my last.

I looked at the Rooneys' roof, which I once climbed out on but then I couldn't climb back in, until the Fire Department came and helped me. I looked at Pearson's Drug Store, where they once said my mom had to pay them eighty dollars when I threw a ball in the air that I almost caught.

I looked at the lot next to Albert's house, where I once and for all
learned to tell which was poison ivy.
I looked at my school, where even Ms. Knoop, the teacher I once
spilled the goldfish bowl on, said she'd miss me.

I looked at my special places where a lot of different things
happened—not just different bad but different good.
Like winning that sack race.
Like finding that flashlight.
Like spitting farther than Jack three times in a row.